With loving memories
of Florence Regina Levy White
who, from the day Ann was born, read poetry to her
and of Albert White
who chose many of Ann's favorite early books.

First Edition First Printing

Printed in China

AN SSL MSL BOOK

Designed by
Hwin&LittleBearPress LLC

Parsley

Written by
ANN LEWIN-BENHAM

Illustrated by
KAREN BUSCH HOLMAN

Peter pulled up my parsley,
My curly parsley,
I grew my parsley from seeds.
But Peter pulled up my parsley.
He must have thought it was weeds.

PARSLEY
PARSLEY

Impatiently I waited
For the cold
Which was belated
To depart.

Then the crocuses
Were done
So I knew
The time had come
To start.

I chose a level place
Rich with worms
And lots of space
And sun

And worked it
With a hoe
Back and forth
And to and fro
‘Til it was done.

But Peter pulled up my parsley,
My curly parsley.
The package said Guaranteed.
And Peter pulled up my parsley.
It must have looked like a weed.

Biennial
HERB
Height: 10-12 inches
Full Sun, Part Sun
Parsley
ORGANIC SEEDS
Extra Curly
PACK OF 50 SEEDS
Guaranteed!

I made furrows, not too deep,
And the dirt
Lay in a heap
Beside each row

Parsley
Extra Curly
Guaranteed

And every row was straight
Where the seeds
Would germinate
And start to grow.

Then I spread them in,
Not too thick
Not too thin
And one by one.
I pushed the dirt back on
And gently tamped it down.
Then I was done.

PARSLEY
Parsley
ORGANIC SEEDS
Extra Curly

But Peter pulled up my parsley,
My curly parsley
I'd been so careful to weed.
Yes, Peter pulled up my parsley.
He pulled it up indeed!

PARSLEY
PARSLEY

Each morning I ran out
To see if any sprout was there,
And as the days got hotter
I sprinkled lots of water
Everywhere.
The days were very slow
My seeds would never grow
Or so it seemed . . .

PARSLEY
PARSLEY

Then *one day*

There they were

Very small but very sure

And green,

Tender little things

On skinny little stalks

With “wings.”

Each day
The plants would rise
And right before my eyes
They grew
A green and curly bed
Just like the package said
They'd do.

The stalks were very thin
But leaves were filling in
Not like the tiny bunch
They'd been.
And I had never seen
Anything that looked
So green.

I looked at them all day.

When puppy said, “Bow wow!

Let’s play!”

“Not now!”

Was all that I

Could say.

Waiting time was past.
In no time just a glance
Showed full and bushy plants
No longer very small
My parsley plants were thick
And tall,
Growing up so high
I wondered if they soon
Might touch the sky.

But Peter pulled up my parsley
My curly parsley
That grew so high and strong.
Yes, Peter pulled up my parsley!
Did he know he'd done wrong?

PARSLEY
RSLEY

Then Daddy came to look
And Mommy even took
A snip

To give the salad texture
And just a little extra
ZIP!

But Peter pulled up my parsley,
My curly parsley,
And dinner soon would be on.
I ran to cut some for mother . . .

. . . but all my parsley was gone!
Parsley, my curly parsley,
Was strewn across the lawn!
The greens were widely scattered
Everywhere all about:
"What happened to my parsley!"
Was all that I could shout.
PETER HAD PULLED UP MY PARSLEY
He was sitting on the bed
And all around Peter was parsley
Even on Peter's head!

PARSLEY
Peter

How to Grow Parsley

If you start with seeds:
Help your seeds GERMINATE, the first step in a plant's growth.
Seeds germinate when:
You put the seeds in soil -- ½" deep and 6 inches apart.

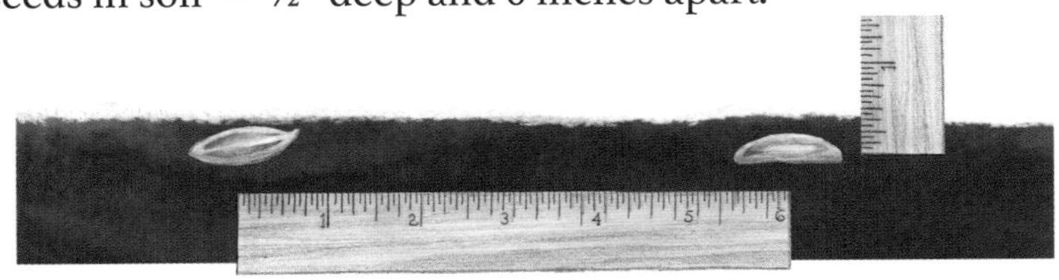

You sprinkle water on the soil.
You choose a place with warmth from sunlight or, if indoors, lightbulbs.
OOPS! Seeds don't grow!
Too deep! The seeds used up their energy . . .
Too much water! The seeds drowned.

Four environmental factors:

Light Water Oxygen Temperature

While seeds germinate, they absorb water through their seed coat.
Before the leaves sprout, the seeds are nourished by food stored within themselves.

All these words mean germinate:
SPROUT SPRING UP SHOOT DEVELOP GROW SWELL PUT FORTH BUD

Planting, Tending and Harvesting

1. Planting in the ground: Parsley likes it COOL!
   1) Plant seeds 5 weeks before the last frost.
   (If there is no frost, plant before it is too hot.)
   2) Plant seeds in soil, ½" deep and 6" apart.
   3) Sprinkle water on the soil. *Do not overwater!*

2. Planting in containers: Parsley's taproot is *long*!
   Use containers about 8" deep (indoors or out).

3. Tending your plants once leaves sprout:
   1) Give each seedling about 1 square inch of space.
   2) Thin the bed by removing straggly sprouts.
   3) Pinch out small stems to make the plant bushier.
   4) For more space, move some plants to a 2nd bed.

4. Parsley likes well-drained soil. Let the top inch of soil dry out.
   Do not overwater!

5. Parsley grows all summer long.
   1) The more you cut stems, the more parsley grows.
   2) Harvest by cutting parsley's old outer leaves first.

6. At season's end, don't uproot! Parsley often re-grows a 2nd year.

7. Parsley has a sweet tangy taste and is beautiful.
   Use parsley to decorate food or add it to flower arrangements.

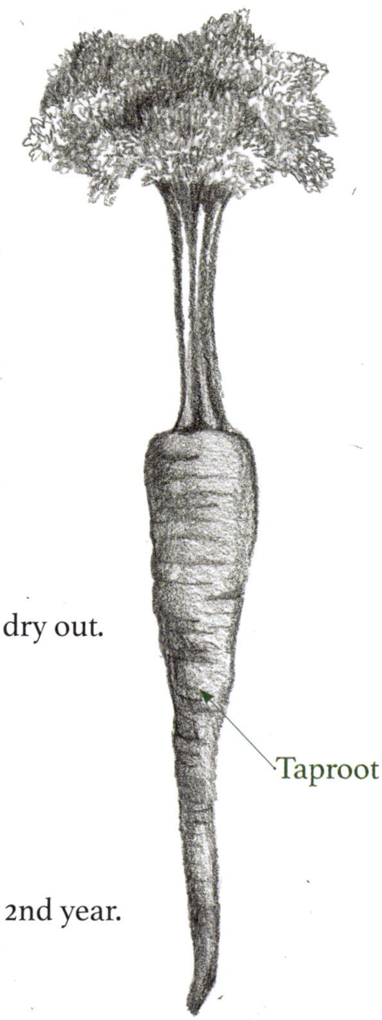

This book's binding is *section sewn and hard bound*, highly durable and made for a lot of handling.

In printing this book, 1) products were made from responsibly managed forests; 2) vegetable soy-based inks, less harmful than petroleum-based products, were used; 3) no traditional film or associated chemicals were used; and 4) electricity and water were subject to waste reduction controls.

The International Council of Toy Industries Care has certified that persons working on this book were treated ethically and that working conditions during production were respectful and humane.

SCS Global Services, established in 1959 with today 2,400 sites worldwide, inspected, tested, and certified that no hazardous substances were detected in the inks, papers, glues, glosses and lamination processes used in this book.

The Forest Stewardship Council and the International Council of Toy Industries Care both certified that the company printing *Parsley* met all their standards.

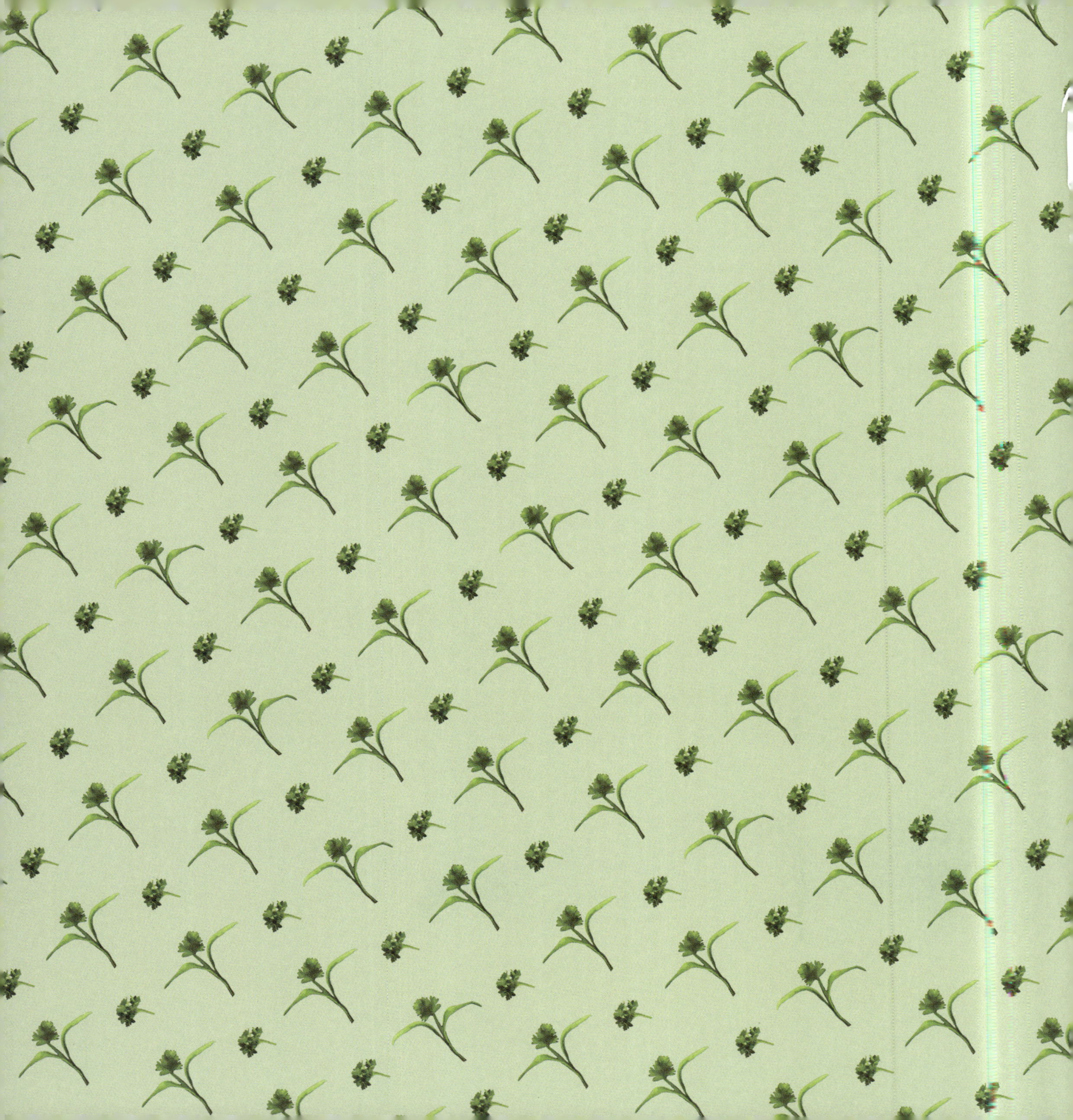